REMARKABLE PEOPLE

Al Gore

by James De Medeiros

Published by Weigl Publishers Inc.
350 5th Avenue, Suite 3304, PMB 6G
New York, NY 10118-0069

Website: www.weigl.com

Library of Congress Cataloging-in-Publication Data

De Medeiros, James, 1975-
  Al Gore / James De Medeiros.
     p. cm. -- (Remarkable people)
  Includes bibliographical references and index.
  ISBN 978-1-59036-992-0 (hard cover : alk. paper) -- ISBN 978-1-59036-993-7 (soft
cover : alk. paper)
1. Gore, Albert, 1948---Juvenile literature. 2. Vice-Presidents--United States--
Biography--Juvenile literature. 3. Legislators--United States--Biography--Juvenile
literature. 4. United States. Congress. Senate--Biography--Juvenile literature. 5.
Presidential candidates--United States--Biography--Juvenile literature. 6.
Environmentalists--United States--Biography--Juvenile literature. I. Title.
  E840.8.G65D4 2009
  973.929092--dc22
  [B]

                              2008003952

Printed in the United States of America
1 2 3 4 5 6 7 8 9 0 12 11 10 09 08

Editor: Danielle LeClair
Design: Terry Paulhus

Contents

Who Is Al Gore?

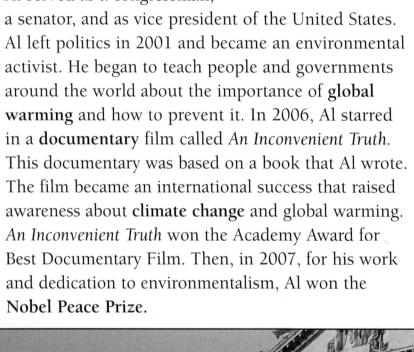

Al Gore is an **environmental activist.** He is also one of the most successful politicians of his time. Al entered politics in 1976 as a congressman in the U.S. House of Representatives. In his years in government, Al served as a congressman,

> **"Not only does human-caused global warming exist, but it is also growing more and more dangerous, and at a pace that has now made it a planetary emergency."**

a senator, and as vice president of the United States. Al left politics in 2001 and became an environmental activist. He began to teach people and governments around the world about the importance of **global warming** and how to prevent it. In 2006, Al starred in a **documentary** film called *An Inconvenient Truth.* This documentary was based on a book that Al wrote. The film became an international success that raised awareness about **climate change** and global warming. *An Inconvenient Truth* won the Academy Award for Best Documentary Film. Then, in 2007, for his work and dedication to environmentalism, Al won the **Nobel Peace Prize.**

Growing Up

lbert A. Gore, Jr., was born in Washington, DC, on March 31, 1948. Al grew up in two places. During the school year, Al, his older sister Nancy, and his parents lived in a hotel in Washington to be near his father's work. When the school year ended, Al and his family returned home to their farm in Carthage, Tennessee.

Al's father was Albert Arnold Gore, Sr., who was a **Democratic** congressman and a senator for Tennessee. Al's mother was Pauline LaFon Gore. Pauline was one of the first women in the southern United States to practice law. From an early age, Al was involved in the world of politics. As a little boy, Al's father would let Al listen in on phone conversations he had with President John F. Kennedy. Al's mother would often invite powerful people and politicians to dinner parties. Young Al listened to them talk about the important topics of the time. Growing up surrounded by politics and politicians made Al aware of the world around him and how he might be able to make a difference.

Al grew up as one of the only children living at the Fairfax hotel in Washington, DC.

Get to Know Tennessee

ANIMAL
Raccoon

STATE FLAG

FLOWER
Iris

Tennessee became the 16th state to enter the Union on June 1, 1796, with a population of 77,000 people.

The name Tennessee comes from the Yuchi Indian word, *Tanasi*, meaning "the meeting place."

Tennessee is often called the volunteer state.

Tennessee has nine members in the House of Representatives.

Nashville is the state capital.

As a child, Al lived in both Washington, DC, and Nashville, Tennessee. There are more than 500 miles (805 kilometers) between these cities. The cities are very different. Imagine spending most of your life in one place because of your parents' work, and then going home for the summer. What challenges would you face if you lived in two different cities?

Practice Makes Perfect

As the son of a U.S. politician, world issues were always being discussed in Al's family. In fact, as a young boy Al received daily lessons from his father in political **philosophy**. Even Al's classmates at St. Alban's School in Washington knew that he would achieve success. Under his high school graduation picture, Al's classmates wrote, "Al is frighteningly good at many things....It probably won't be long before he reaches the top."

With his life-long interest in politics, Al decided to study government at Harvard University. After Al graduated from Harvard in 1969, he enlisted in the United States Army. Al served as a military reporter in the Vietnam War. When Al left the army, he took a job as a reporter in Nashville, Tennessee. While working as a reporter, Al realized he wanted to follow in his father's footsteps and pursue politics. Al continued to work as a reporter and enrolled at Vanderbilt University to study law and theology, or religion. In 1976, Al's dream of entering politics took a big step forward.

Al was a successful politician. He was the first senator in Tennessee to win the votes of every county.

When Al was in law school, a longtime congressman from Tennessee announced his retirement from the House of Representatives. Al quit law school to campaign for the seat. He won the election and was re-elected three more times.

In 1985, after nine years as a congressman, Al became the senator for Tennessee. Then in 1992, Democratic presidential candidate Bill Clinton named Al as his vice-presidential running mate. Clinton and Gore won the election. For eight years, Al served as the vice president. In 2000, Al decided to run for president. In the election, Al won more of the **popular votes,** but he lost the **Electoral College** vote. Al lost the presidential election to George W. Bush.

▧ Bill Clinton and Al Gore were the first Democratic president and vice-president to win back-to-back elections since 1934.

Key Events

When Al was attending university in 1968, he took a class about environmentalism and global warming from professor and **oceanographer** Roger Revelle. In his class, Roger spoke about how **carbon dioxide** levels were increasing and how this was harming the atmosphere. This was a lesson that stayed with Al. It shaped his ideas about the environment forever.

In 1988, Al wrote a book called *Earth in the Balance*. Al wrote about the need for humankind to focus on saving the environment. The book did well, becoming a *New York Times* bestseller. Yet, there were many political and business leaders who refused to believe that there was a threat to the environment.

Al left politics in 2000 and dedicated his life to environmentalism. In 2006, he wrote and starred in the Academy Award-winning documentary *An Inconvenient Truth*. For his work and dedication to the environment, Al shared the 2007 Nobel Peace Prize Award with the Intergovernmental Panel on Climate Change (IPCC). The IPCC is a group of scientists that evaluate the risk of climate change caused by human activity.

■ The Nobel Prize comes with a prize of $1.5 million. Al donated his share of that prize to the Alliance for Climate Protection.

Thoughts from Al

As a child, Al wanted to change the world. Here are some of the things he has said about his interests and his life.

Al knows the importance of issues and voting.

"A vote is not just a piece of paper, a vote is a human voice, a statement of human principle, and we must not let those voices be silenced."

Al explains how much his father meant to him.

"My father was the greatest man I ever knew in my life."

Al talks about protecting the environment.

"We must change the way we view and treat the world around us. We must conserve energy, invest in environmentally sound products and processes, and increase environmental education."

Al talks about working to stop climate change.

"If you want to go fast, go alone, if you want to go far, go together."

Al talks about the future.

"Future generations may well have occasion to ask themselves, "What were our parents thinking? Why didn't they wake up when they had a chance?" We have to hear that question from them, now."

Al enjoys being a father.

"Fatherhood is frustrating and humbling. But it can also be one of the greatest joys that a man can know."

What Is an Environmental Activist?

Environmental activists are people who are concerned about the environment. They want to preserve and protect Earth from harmful activity. Environmental activists are concerned with many issues. These issues include **toxic waste**, pollution, **ozone depletion**, energy **conservation**, and climate change.

Al has spent more that 30 years as an environmental activist. He spent much of his time as a politician working to improve the environment. As vice president, Al became well known around the world. He used his influence to speak and write about enviromental issues. Now, Al devotes all of his time to this cause. He is a successful environmental activist and is one of the most powerful voices in the world speaking out against climate change. Al has lectured, written books, raised money, and made documentaries to educate the world about this issue.

▨ After Al won the Nobel Peace Prize, many people hoped he would run for president in 2008.

Environmental Activists 101

Ralph Nader (1934–)

Cause: Consumer rights
Achievements: Ralph Nader is a well-known political activist. Ralph began his career as a lawyer. In 1961, he taught history and government at the University of Hartford. He was first seen as an activist defending consumer rights. As the years passed, Ralph expanded his role as an activist for democratic government, humanitarianism, and environmentalism. His strong stand on issues has driven him to run for president

Caroline Lucas (1960–)

Cause: Environmentalism
Achievements: Caroline Lucas is a member of the Green Party of England. She entered politics after spending many years as an activist. Since 2004, she has been a member of the Women's Environmental Network organization. The organization educates women about their role in saving the environment. She has written on many environmental topics. Other issues important to her include human rights and peace.

Peter Garrett (1953–)

Cause: Environmentalism
Achievements: Peter Garrett is the Australian Minister for the Environment. Before becoming a politician, he was the singer for the rock band, Midnight Oil. He studied law and arts in university, and was an environmental activist. Peter served as president of Australian Conservation Foundation before entering politics. In 2004, Peter was elected to the Australian House of Representatives as a member of the Australian Labor Party.

Robert F. Kennedy (1954–)

Cause: Environmentalism
Achievements: Robert F. Kennedy, Jr., was born in Washington, DC. Robert earned a political science degree from Harvard University before going to law school and focusing on environmental law and speaks about environmental issues at events such as the 2007 Live Earth show. Robert has been a university professor of environmental law since 1987.

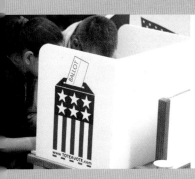

Politicians

Politicians are people who make up the government that runs a city, a state, or a country. In the United States, politicians are chosen in elections. During an election, registered voters cast **ballots** for the candidate of their choice. The candidate with the most votes wins the election. It is the job of a politician to make laws that support the issues and concerns of the people who elect them.

Influences

Al has had two main influences in his life. They are his faith and his family. Both of these influences continue to guide Al every day.

Growing up, Al's family would attend church every Sunday. One Sunday, the family would attend his mother's church. The next Sunday, they would attend his father's. Attending different churches helped Al learn the importance of respecting people regardless of their background or beliefs. He learned to be open-minded and accepting. Al's interest in religion was so strong that he decided to study theology after returning from the Vietnam War.

Family life and fatherhood are very important to Al. In 1994, he hosted a national conference called "Family Reunion III: Men in Children's Lives" to discuss government policies on family.

When Al met his wife Tipper at his high school graduation dance, he knew that he wanted to start a life and family with her. Tipper has influenced Al more than any other person. Al gives Tipper a great deal of credit for helping him become the person he is today.

His parents, his faith, and his wife have helped Al see and understand the world in different ways. Their influence provides Al with the inspiration to succeed as a politician and as an environmental activist.

DR. ROGER REVELLE

Another important influence in Al's life was Dr. Roger Revelle. Roger was a scientist, an explorer, a war veteran, a scientific advisor, and the teacher who inspired Al. Roger was an early environmental activist. He spoke strongly about issues, such as the environment, education, agriculture, and world population. Roger was appointed to advise President John F. Kennedy about scientific matters. Roger may be best known for his early prediction of global warming and his recognition of greenhouse gases.

In 1990, Roger was awarded the National Medal of Science for being "the grandfather of the greenhouse effect."

Overcoming Obstacles

Al has faced many challenges as a politician and environmentalist. These challenges affected both Al's family life and his career.

On April 3, 1989, Al's life changed when his 6-year-old son, Albert, was seriously injured. Al and his son were leaving a Baltimore Orioles baseball game when Albert let go of his father's hand and stepped into traffic. Albert was hit by a car. The injuries were severe. Al gave up his plan to run in the 1992 presidential election. Instead of traveling across the country campaigning, Al stayed home to take care of his son. During that time, Al began writing *Earth in the Balance*.

Al was one of the youngest politicians to ever seek the nomination for president.

The biggest obstacle in Al's career was his loss in the presidential election in 2000. The loss was a very difficult one for Al to accept. To win the presidency, a candidate must win 269 electoral votes. Al won 266 and George W. Bush won 271. Al demanded the votes be carefully recounted.

There was a great deal of confusion over the voting, especially in Florida. After the recount of all the votes in that state, the Florida supreme court made a decision that gave the votes to Al. However, the United States supreme court reversed the state court's ruling. It gave the election to George W. Bush. Al accepted the loss knowing he had done everything he could to become president.

In the 2000 presidential race, Al won 500,000 more votes than his rival George W. Bush. This made Al the first presidential candidate since 1888 to lose an election even though he won more of the popular vote.

Achievements and Successes

As an environmental activist, Al has won many awards. Al was awarded the Nobel Peace Prize, an Emmy Award, and two Quill Awards. The Quill Award is given to recognize inspired writing. Al won for his books *An Inconvienent Truth* and *The Assault on Reason*. The Emmy Award was for Outstanding Creative Achievement in Interactive Television for Current TV. Al was awarded one of the most highly respected international awards, the Nobel Peace Prize, along with the Intergovernmental Panel on Climate Change. Al received this award for being the person most responsible for informing the world about man-made climate change and for providing ideas on how to reverse these changes.

▬ The Academy Award winning film *An Inconvenient Truth* was an international success. It earned more that $24 million worldwide. It is the third highest-earning documentary in history.

In 2005, Al was awarded a Webby Awards' Lifetime Achievement Award for the important role he played in the advancement of the Internet. During his time as a politician, Al influenced government and business leaders, and helped create laws that made the Internet available to the public. Al advises companies including Apple Inc. and the Current TV network.

As the head of an organization called the Alliance for Climate Protection, Al helped organize and put on Live Earth. This was a 24-hour worldwide musical concert to raise awareness for environmental protection.

SAVE OUR SELVES (SOS)

On July 7, 2007, Live Earth brought together 150 musical acts. The concerts were shown around the world. They were performed to raise awareness about the climate crisis. Live Earth introduced a three-year plan to inspire companies, governments, and individuals to combat global warming. Live Earth asked people around the world to sign a pledge to help put an end to climate change. To learn more about Live Earth, the worldwide concerts, and the pledge, visit **www.liveearth.org**.

Write a Biography

A person's life story can be the subject of a book. This kind of book is called a biography. Biographies describe the lives of remarkable people, such as those who have achieved great success or have done important things to help others. These people may be alive today, or they may have lived many years ago. Reading a biography can help you learn more about a remarkable person.

At school, you might be asked to write a biography. First, decide who you want to write about. You can choose a political figure, such as Al Gore, or any other person you find interesting. Then, find out if your library has any books about this person. Learn as much as you can about him or her. Write down the key events in this person's life. What was this person's childhood like? What has he or she accomplished? What are his or her goals? What makes this person special or unusual?

A concept web is a useful research tool. Read the questions in the following concept web. Answer the questions in your notebook. Your answers will help you write your biography review.

- Where does this individual currently reside?
- Does he or she have a family?

- What did you learn from the books you read in your research?
- Would you suggest these books to others?
- Was anything missing from these books?

- Where and when was this person born?
- Describe his or her parents, siblings, and friends.
- Did this person grow up in unusual circumstances?

Your Opinion

Adulthood

Childhood

WRITING A BIOGRAPHY

Main Accomplishments

Help and Obstacles

Work and Preparation

- What is this person's life's work?
- Has he or she received awards or recognition for accomplishments?
- How have this person's accomplishments served others?

- What was this person's education?
- What was his or her work experience?
- How does this person work; what is or was the process he or she uses or used?

- Did this individual have a positive attitude?
- Did he or she receive help from others?
- Did this person have a mentor?
- Did this person face any hardships?
- If so, how were the hardships overcome?

Timeline

YEAR	AL GORE	WORLD EVENTS
1948	Albert A. Gore is born on March 31 in Washington, DC.	The presidential conventions are televised for the first time.
1965	Al enters Harvard University.	The U.S. announces it will send 3,500 troops to Vietnam.
1970	Al marries Mary Elizabeth Aitcheson, also called Tipper.	The Environmental Protection Agency is created.
1976	Al announces his candidacy for U.S. Representative for the state of Tennessee.	The leader of China, Mao Zedong, dies.
1992	Al is elected vice president of the United States.	The Bosnian War begins. The war lasts for more than three years.
2000	Al loses one of the closest presidential elections in history to George W. Bush.	Hillary Rodham Clinton is elected to the senate.
2007	Along with the Intergovernmental Panel on Climate Change, Al wins the Nobel Peace Prize.	Tony Blair resigns after 10 years as British prime minister.

Further Research

How can I find out more about Al Gore?

Most libraries have computers that connect to a database that contains information on books and articles about different subjects. You can input a key word and find material on the person, place, or thing you want to learn more about. The computer will provide you with a list of books in the library that contain information on the subject you searched for. Non-fiction books are arranged numerically, using their call number. Fiction books are organized alphabetically by the author's last name.

Websites

To learn more about Al's work as an environmental activist, visit www.algore.com

To discover more about the U.S. politics and politicians, visit www.kids.gov
Click "K-5" or "6-8." Choose "Government."

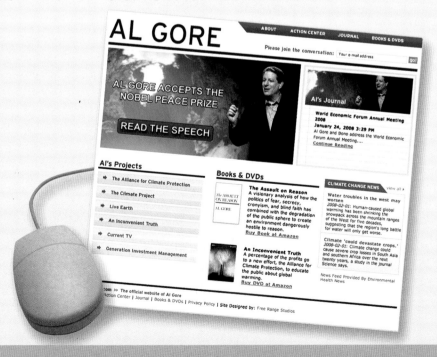

Words to Know

ballots: pieces of paper on which people who are voting enter their choices

carbon dioxide: a colorless, odorless gas made up of carbon and oxygen

climate change: the process by which greenhouse gases are believed to be causing changes in Earth's climate

conservation: to protect something from destruction

Democratic: one of the two major political parties in the United States

documentary: a film based on real facts and events

Electoral College: a group of people chosen by the voters in each state to elect the president and vice president of the United States

environmental activist: a person who works to preserve and protect Earth and all its species from harm

global warming: a warming of Earth's temperature due to air pollution and the destruction of the ozone layer

greenhouse gases: gases in the atmosphere that trap the Sun's energy and contribute to rising temperatures

Nobel Peace Prize: an international prize to recognize the person, people, or groups who make an important impact in their fields

oceanographer: a scientist who studies life in the ocean

ozone depletion: the thinning of a protective layer of oxygen that surrounds Earth

philosophy: the study of the nature of life, truth, knowledge, and other important human matters

popular votes: the total number of votes cast by eligible voters

toxic waste: waste that contains or releases poisonous substances in large enough amounts to threaten human health or the environment

Index